J.C. Hsyu: For Amah

Kenard Pak: For Dad

Published in the US by Nobrow (US) Inc.
Printed in Belgium on FSC assured paper.
ISBN: 978-1-909263-41-3

Order from www.flyingeyebooks.com

FSC
www.fsc.org
MIX
Paper from
responsible sources
FSC® C101807

THE DINNER THAT COOKED ITSELF

J.C. Hsyu and Kenard Pak

Flying Eye Books

London - New York

Long ago in China there lived an honest,
respectful and hard-working man named Tuan.
As a child he had lost his parents and his kind neighbours
Old Lin and Madame Lin had raised him instead.

When Tuan was old enough to live by himself he
moved into a small house with a small field,
but he was lonely and he longed for a wife.
And so, Old Lin and Madame Lin hired a matchmaker.

First, the matchmaker suggested the farmer's beautiful daughter.
But she had been born in the Year of the **Tiger**, and Tuan
had been born in the Year of the **Dog**. With a cat and a dog fighting
for room under such a small roof there would never be peace.

Second, the matchmaker suggested the silk weaver's lovely daughter. But her name contained the character for **Wood**, and Tuan's name contained the character for **Earth**. With Wood and Earth fighting for room under such a small roof there would never be growth.

Third, the matchmaker suggested the scholar's pretty daughter.
She had been born in the year of the **Rabbit**, a good match for the year of the **Dog**.
And her name contained the character for **Fire**, which creates **Earth**.
But Tuan was just a humble clerk and too poor for her parents to approve.

Despite his loneliness, Tuan continued to work hard. At sunrise he went
to work in the magistrate's court, and when he came home he tended to
the vegetables in his field until the sun went down.

One night, Tuan stayed out later than usual,
gathering cabbages. Finally, he sat down to rest and watch
the moonrise. The moon was bright and in its glow Tuan noticed
a large stone by his feet. He leaned closer and saw that the large stone was...

...a large snail!

"What luck!"
Tuan exclaimed, picking up the snail.
"Are you hungry? I'll look after you!"
He had never seen a snail this big and surely
such a rare creature meant good fortune.

At home he placed the snail in a large jar with some succulent cabbage leaves.

The next night, a very curious thing happened...
Returning home after another long day's work, Tuan found his table
already set with a dinner of cooked rice and vegetables.

"It must have been dear Madame Lin," Tuan thought,
as he happily munched on crispy bean sprouts.

But Madame Lin had been working on her farm all day.
She didn't do it!

The next, next night another curious thing happened...
Tuan came home and found little fried balls of pork,
a plump chicken stewed with plums and a hearty beef noodle
soup next to the steaming bowls of rice and vegetables.

It was even more delicious than the dinner from the day before.
"Who is being so kind to me?" Tuan wondered as he ate.

"It must have been the scholar's daughter who has taken pity on my loneliness and cooked this for me!"

But the scholar's daughter had been practising her calligraphy. She didn't do it!

Tuan was very confused. He went home and fed the snail some fresh, crunchy bamboo shoots.

"I don't know who is being so kind to me, but if I am lucky enough to eat well then you should too, my friend."

The night after that yet another curious thing happened.
When Tuan came home his table was covered with even more food!

Now more than ever, he wanted to find
out how his dinners were cooking themselves.

The following evening Tuan came home early and hid near the table.
Then the most curious thing of all happened...

...a beautiful woman, in long silk robes that flowed like water, climbed out of the jar!

"Hello!"
Tuan cried out.

"Who are you?"

"Oh!" she said in surprise. "My name is White Wave and I am a fairy. The Lord of Heaven took pity on you because you lost your parents when you were very young and live alone in a small house with a small field...

...Because you work hard and are honest and respectful, I was sent to look after you until you became rich and married a wife."

Then she looked sad.

"But mortals cannot see fairies in their true form and so I must leave."

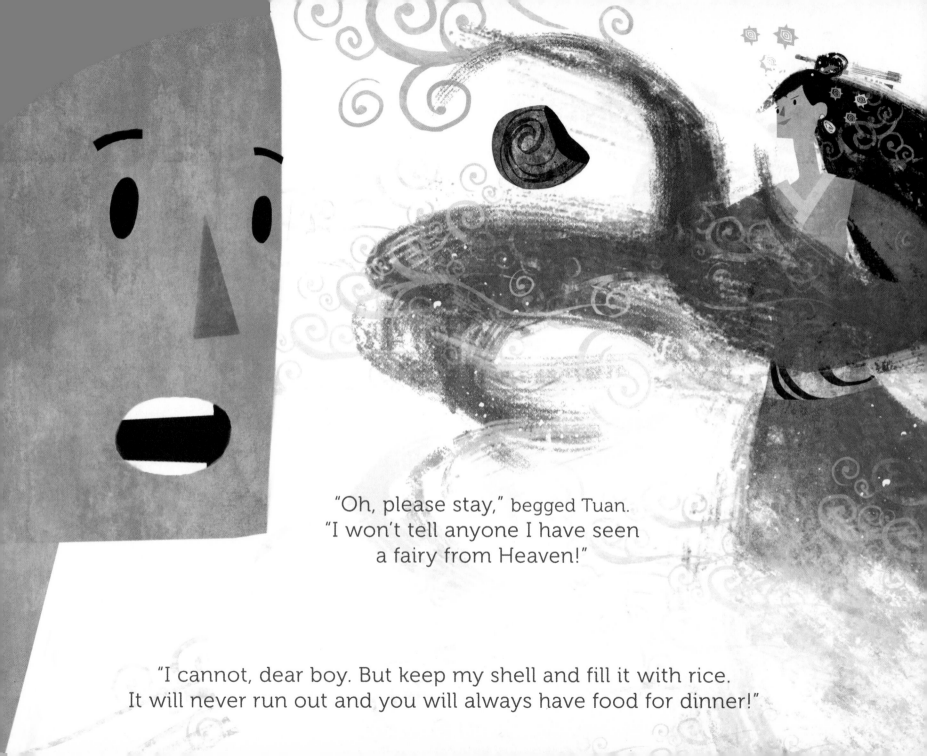

"Oh, please stay," begged Tuan.
"I won't tell anyone I have seen
a fairy from Heaven!"

"I cannot, dear boy. But keep my shell and fill it with rice.
It will never run out and you will always have food for dinner!"

The sky grew dark and a heavy rain began to fall.
White Wave ran to the door, spread her arms and
flew away on the mighty gusts of wind.

Out of gratitude, Tuan built a shrine to the fairy and her shell.

From that day on he never failed to pay his respects to White Wave and the Lord of Heaven and he never missed a dinner.

Although Tuan never became wealthy, he continued
to work hard at court and in his field.

In time he became a magistrate and married a woman
who was born in a matching year and had matching characters in her name.

They loved each other very much and lived happily together.

Can you read Chinese?

In our story, there are Chinese characters for **Tiger**, **Dog**, **Wood**, **Earth**, **Fire**, and **Rabbit**. Did you spot the Chinese characters in the book? Look again!

Chinese characters are very, very old. The first ones were written long before Tuan, Old Lin and Madame Lin were born. They began as pictures of the objects being described, but today they symbolize everything from objects to sounds or ideas.

Each character is made up of brushstrokes. The art of writing Chinese characters is called Chinese calligraphy. Chinese calligraphers use ink brushes to draw the characters.

書法
Calligraphy

蝸牛
Snail

Today, there are thousands and thousands of Chinese characters.
Here are characters for some of the food in the biggest, tastiest dinner that White Wave made!

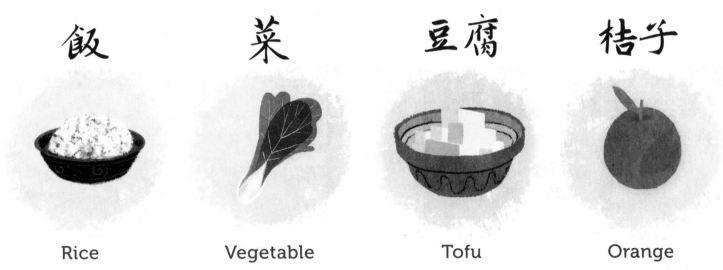

飯

菜

豆腐

桔子

Rice

Vegetable

Tofu

Orange